Denise DeCarolis

I0552572

THE PROTECTORS OF THE KNIGHT

By

Denise DeCarolis

1

Denise DeCarolis

Denise DeCarolis

About The Author

Denise DeCarolis is an adventurous person and avid writer who was born and raised in Brooklyn, New York. Graduating from high school with English and Science as her majors, she started her work career as a home health aide and then as a school bus monitor caring for special needs children, while transporting them to and from school.

Denise discovered her love of writing while helping her son with an English assignment in school. Together, they put together a wonderful story that helped him achieve a high mark. That opened up her creativity and kickstarted the creative process that became the Protectors of the Knight.

Denise is presently retired, residing in upstate New York, and spends her day writing and pursuing her hobbies, which include arts, crafts, making wreaths, cooking for her family, and driving around to new locations, especially waterfalls, so she can capture nature through the lens of her camera. Drawing her inspiration from her family, she is a proud mother of four and an even prouder grandmother of five. She's also an animal lover and, just like any creative soul, loves music. She has a fascination with dragon figurines and collects them enthusiastically

Protectors of the Knight is her first official publication, It's a story that takes its readers on a stunning adventure in another world.

Dedication

I am lovingly dedicating this book to my children and grandchildren. I love you;

you are my inspiration

Table Of Contents

Denise DeCarolis

THE DREAM

His quest starts in a dream. It was a beautiful, starlit evening. As he slept, the Knight dreamt of his future. He did not know this dream would change his life in ways he could never imagine. He was only a servant of the king, but in his dream, he felt he was more important.

His name is Torrance, a young man, large with broad shoulders, long sandy brown hair, and gleaming green eyes. He is a Knight; he is quick with a sword and has a wit quicker than his hand. His eyes are as sharp as a hawk with a bow and arrow. His dream is of a man, not just any man, but a powerful man. As the dream continued, he envisioned himself walking through a field with trees in full bloom. The countryside was cascading with flowers of every color he could imagine. Animals were in abundance, birds were chirping and flying high in the sky, and fish were swimming in the stream. To him, it sounded like music, and watching the animals, it seemed like nature's ballet.

8

He walked for a long time, or so it seemed in his dream until Torrance came to a place in his mind that seemed to make him feel safe. He saw this man off in the distance, calling the Knight to his side. The man was not an ordinary man, for there was an aura about him, something that he had never felt before; it was magical. Torrance knew this man held the key to things in his life that he could not remember or had faded with age. The vision of a man made him feel important, but he did not know why. He knew something was about to change his life forever. He could hear the man telling him they had to have a meeting. "Come to the forest. I will be waiting," the Knight heard as his dream began to fade.

His mind raced, and then he awoke with a jolt that shot through his body. "Hello," Torrance called out but realized he was alone in his quarters with only a soft, gentle breeze blowing on him from the open balcony, which he thought he had closed when he went to sleep that evening.

9

As he awoke, his dream replayed in his head; the dream of a man, only he knew he was more than a man. A wizard! Torrance exclaimed to himself. Yes, that is what this man is. He recanted in his mind. I must be a fool, Torrance thought to himself. There were no such things as wizards! He was told as a young lad stories that had magic and wizards in them. But that was all they were, just stories, so why do I feel this man would be a wizard? He continued to debate with himself. He then decided to put these thoughts out of his mind and go on with the day as usual. He could not, though. It did not seem like a normal day.

He remembered the wizard told him that they would meet and Torrance would be given instructions as to why the wizard needed him. Torrance washed his face, trying to get the dream out of his mind, but it kept replaying repeatedly.

DAY ONE

Torrance was now fully awake but not able to shake the visions of the past night's dream from his mind. He decided to take a walk in the brisk morning air. He walked down into the courtyard, through the meadow to the top of a knoll, where he had played as a young boy. He knew he could see for miles, or so it had seemed to him. He climbed to the top of the knoll only to find that his dream had come true.

THE MEETING

Under a huge weeping willow tree, there he was, a tall, thin figure of a man wearing long purple and silver robes and carrying a staff. His silver hair matched his beard, but his face did not look old. It was more of a look of confidence gained through experience, which had taken its toll on a younger man.

The Wizard Orian greeted Torrance with a gesture as if he had been expected and was long overdue. Torrance walked over to the wizard, but he did not feel that he was in danger. Instead, he felt as if he belonged in this spot at this very moment in time.

"I am Orian," the wizard said as he extended his hand to the knight. Torrance started to introduce himself to Orian but was soon interrupted. "Please have a seat," Orian said. Torrance took a seat on the grass under the tree. Orian sat across from him. "Do you think this meeting happened by chance?" asked Orian. "There is no need for you to introduce yourself to me, my boy. I have known you since you were born."

"How is that possible?" asked Torrance. "I have never met you before now," Orian explained that he was the consultant for the previous king, King Artis. "You would not remember him, for he was killed in a jousting contest when you were a mere two years of age. Your mother, Lenore, was his chambermaid, and you, my boy, are his son."

With this statement, Torrance was taken aback; he had not known his Father, and his mother never spoke of him. "King Artis and your mother could not be married despite their love for one another, for she was not of royal blood. King Artis never married; he knew that no one in the Kingdom could bring him the happiness he had known with your mother. Their secret was kept hidden from you and all others in the Kingdom except his brother Gavin. Your Uncle, King Gavin, kept you close but did not reveal your identity to a single soul, for you are the next in line, heir to the throne. This was one of the stipulations King Artis and his brother agreed upon, even though your parents were not married. I can see by the look in your eyes, Torrance, that you could not have known that the King is your Uncle," Orian proclaimed, "but King Gavin, the good man that he is, made sure you were trained in the proper style befitting a knight, for these were your father's dying wishes.

'Gavin,' your father said, trying to muster up enough breath to talk, 'please protect my son, train him to be the King he must be.' Gavin agreed, and as your father's breath ran out, the people in the Kingdom sobbed as they watched the passing of your father, their King, but no one ever heard the words spoken between the brothers. Gavin took his place on the throne the next day. Your mother was so heartbroken she could not bear to stay in this castle but remained here for your sake.

King Gavin ruled the Kingdom in the way your father outlined in his last wishes. One day, that all changed. King Gavin started to change, and not for the good. He began to make changes in the Kingdom. The people were not happy with the changes; they were forced to work on the King's land, farming and tending to the animals instead of their own land. The King also started to take land and livestock from the people. He took their services and provided no wages; the people had no wages to buy supplies for their families."

The people of Plaitura were in shock that this man they had come to love as their King would do such things. Orian told Torrance that he had become suspicious of the woman the King had taken on as his advisor. "She had a presence about her," Orian said, "an uncomfortable feeling came upon me," he continued, "whenever she was near, chills shook through my body. Amiana hid a secret; she is a sorceress. Her heart is not pure but black as coal. She put a very powerful spell on King Gavin. He fell in love with her, but not of his doing. Her intentions were to control him and take over the Kingdom. I removed the spell that held him in her power, and after I released him, King Gavin did not remember much of what had taken place. I had a very hard time removing her spell," Orian said, "but after I did, he restored the Kingdom back to the way it was. I had to tell the King what had happened, for he needed to know the truth, and that is when she was banished from the Kingdom. She vowed to get even with me that day! I was also banished," Orian told Torrance, "for I know the truth as well. I used a spell of binding around Plaitura to keep her from coming back. That brings us to our meeting today."

"I had to appear to you in a dream, for the use of magic is forbidden. King Gavin feared someone possessing powers would use them to overtake his kingdom again. He did it to protect himself and everyone that lives in Plaitura."

Torrance was bewildered. *Could this be true?* He asked himself. *Am I really the son of a King? What could I offer the kingdom?* He wondered. *Magic spells, an evil sorceress.* Torrance became confused at what he was hearing, yet he continued to listen intensely to what the wizard told him.

"Torrance, this is why we are here," explained Orian. "Do you know of the dragons?" he asked. Torrance replied with a look of disbelief, "Dragons, what dragons? They are a myth to scare bad children." The wizard laughed as he lit his pipe and blew the smoke into Torrance's face. "Do I seem like a myth to you? Or an old man who has lost all of his senses? I can see it in your eyes, the disbelief of what you are hearing, but your heart tells you otherwise. I am the keeper of the dragons. Six are in my charge. I fear there are evil doings in our midst," explained Orian.

"These six dragons are the protectors of the night and the innocent. They are usually obedient, never out of my sight for long, but I fear something is amiss. I have not been able to find them for two days now. It is very, very strange for them not to come when summoned. The dragons are the protectors of all that is good," Orian told Torrance. "This is why I am so concerned and need to finally reveal your true destiny. The six dragons left each possess their own special abilities. I will inform you of each of their names and talents, as I like to call it," said Orian.

Torrance sat there with a look of amazement on his face. Again, he thought to himself and did not know what to believe. Am I here? Am I really the son of a King? Do dragons really exist? Orian called his name to snap him out of his daze. "Torrance," he said, "would you like to start learning all I have to teach you?" Torrance replied, "Yes. Tell me what I have to do to help."

Orian looked at the sky and then stood up. He looked at Torrance and said, "Perhaps we should start tomorrow." Torrance asked, "Why tomorrow? The day is still young." Orian replied, "I have some errands to tend to before we start your training. I have many things to prepare for you, and time is short." Torrance stood up, gave Orian a firm handshake, and then said, "I look forward until the morrow, but I do not know if I can wait that long right now. Tomorrow seems so far away." "Patience, my boy," Orian replied, "You must have patience to succeed. Lack of it can be your downfall."

As Torrance slowly walked back towards the castle, he looked upon the land he calls home. The beauty of the grass, trees, flowers, and the exquisite statues adorning the garden led to the castle stairs. He always felt safe and secure here, even as a little boy. Will all this be mine someday? He asked himself. This kingdom was named Plaitura after the great aunt of King Artis. Queen Plaitura was the wife of the first king of this land, King Garrett. She took this land and turned it into a place of beauty. She sculpted the gardens and designed the castle inside and out. There were six pillars: four on the outer walls, one in the middle of the garden, and the last one, higher than the other pillars, in the center of the castle. This pillar overlooked all of Plaitura and the surrounding lands. The rooms are large and brightly lit, with big archways leading from one room to another and always colorful floral arrangements adorning the hallways. She liked bright places, and this is how the castle has remained since she had it built. A grand ballroom overlooks the lake on the North side of the castle, and on the South side stood a formal dining area almost as large as the ballroom. Torrance had attended many formal affairs here, in his home. As he made his way up the stairs into the front courtyard, he spotted King Gavin.

"Torrance!" the King exclaimed, "There you are; I have been looking for you all day." "Forgive me, Your Majesty," Torrance replied, "I did not sleep very well last night. I thought a long walk would help. Was there something you required of me, my lord?" "No, my boy," replied the king, "I was worried! I missed you at breakfast and again at lunch; I thought you had taken ill. Elaina went to your quarters to see if you were alright. When she came and informed me you were not in your room, I began to think something had happened to you."

Elaina's function in the castle is as a servant to the king. Torrance and Elaina practically grew up together. Elaina was orphaned as an infant, left at the castle, taken in by King Artis, and raised by the servants and chambermaids. She and Torrance would play games, ride horses, and walk in the woods together, sharing many memories. She grew into a beautiful woman.

Elaina stands at a perfect height; her frame is neither too diminutive nor overly imposing, allowing her to command attention with graceful poise. Her flowing locks of blonde hair cascade like sunlit waves, a radiant halo that catches and reflects the light around her, framing her visage. Her hazel eyes dance with a myriad of hues, hinting at depths of emotion and wisdom that only those fortunate enough to know her can fathom.

A warm, inviting smile graces her lips, capable of melting the chilliest of airs and easing the heaviest of hearts. Her smile is a testament to her caring nature and the genuine compassion she carries within.

Torrance apologized once again, "I did not think I would be long and failed to realize time had slipped by so quickly. I should have told someone where I was going. Please forgive me, your Highness."

King Gavin patted Torrance on the shoulder. "Of course, your absence would not have gone unnoticed," he said. "You are very important in the kingdom; after all, you are a knight, the best I have seen in decades, and you are more than capable of handling any situation thrown at you! You must forgive me, my son, for there are times when I look at you and still see that young lad of long ago who desperately needed someone to take you under their wing."

"And I will be forever grateful, my lord!" Torrance replied. "Now, now, little did you know at that time, I needed you as much as you needed me! If there is anyone who should be grateful, it is

I. I believe that makes the score more than ever, wouldn't you say?" Torrance bowed and said with a smile, "Yes, Sire and I will not let this happen again... your Majesty!" With that, King Gavin gave him a hug, patting him on the back, and said, "Then carry on, my boy, carry on."

Torrance was born in this castle; this is the only life he knew. He loved training to be a knight; his plans for the future all laid within this land. One day, his mother requested to be removed from service when he was ten years of age. All that he knew came to a halt that day, for he was only told that his mother was going to the neighboring land of Scandos to be the chambermaid for King Rufus, the ruler of Scandos. Lenore's wishes were for him to continue his knight training under the supervision of King Gavin. Torrance, not wanting to be separated from his mother, begged her to take him with her. Lenore simply smiled at him and said, "Be strong, my son; this is where you belong." She then turned away, tears streaming down her cheeks as she climbed into the awaiting carriage. Lenore could not bear to be in the castle since King Artis died; she stayed there for her son only. Each day she spent in Plaitura, her heart ached. Every room in the castle held memories of a happier day she knew would never come again. Lenore knew she had to leave for Torrance's sake.

As the sun set over the mountains on the West side of Plaitura, the afternoon gave in tonight. Torrance stood on his balcony and watched as the sun slowly faded out of sight. In the back of his mind, he wondered if he would be strong enough to take on the task the Wizard was setting before him. After all, he laughed to himself, and I have never even seen a dragon. Then he remembered the look on Orian's face; he should not be thinking of this in a lighthearted manner. "I have to be serious," he said aloud, then looked around to make sure no one else had heard him. This is my home, and I will do whatever Orian needs me to do in order to protect it and find the missing dragons.

Torrance sat at the table in his quarters, poured himself a tankard of ale, toasted the kingdom, and drank. He sat remembering all that had happened during his childhood. Now, some things started to make sense to him. He watched the day his mother left for Scandos and remembered the look in her eyes as the horse-drawn carriage slowly faded out of his sight. He tried to catch up with his mother's carriage but could not; tears fell from his eyes. He thought he would never get over his mother's leaving. After all, he did not understand until today why she had to go.

Elaina was the only one who understood, for she too was abandoned, just left at the castle. She did not remember her mother or father. They left her at the castle as an infant. Torrance's mother took care of her; the two were like siblings, and on the day Lenore left, Elaina cried, too. Torrance and Elaina held onto each other for strength. They shared their fears and dreams with one another. They talked about what their futures might hold for each of them and the secret desires they had. Torrance always wanted to become a knight, and Elaina always dreamed of being a lady in waiting. Insert description here. He became a knight, but Elaina was only a servant. With sleep closing in on him, Torrance finished his ale and headed for his bed. As he lay there, Torrance drifted off into a peaceful slumber. Soon, the peace turned to distress. In his dreams, he saw the dragons. They were in danger!

DAY TWO·

With a curiosity he needed to satisfy, Torrance arose early. He washed and dressed quickly. He then made his way down the main staircase to the room where the knights ate their morning meal. The room was set off from the main dining area. It has a more intimate feel about it. Torrance liked the feeling of this type of surrounding; only the king and his knights ate in this room. On this morning, however, it was just King Gavin and Torrance in the room. King Gavin was seated in his rightful place at the head of the table, and Torrance was at his right side. "Good morning, Your Majesty," he said as he took his seat. "Good morning, Torrance," the King replied, "I trust you had a better night's sleep." "Yes, Sire, I slept very well, thank you. And you, Highness?" King Gavin laughed, "I slept like a king." This was the normal pleasantry they exchanged almost every morning. They ate a hearty morning meal, and the banter between the Knight and the King was lighthearted as always.

"Torrance, do you have any plans for today?" asked King Gavin. "Yes, Sire," he replied, "I thought I would go on a morning hunt. I hear the stags are plentiful this time of year." "Yes, they are," King Gavin replied, "I hope you have luck; the morning is waiting. The stags are usually by the stream this early. You had better hurry, my boy," he said.

Torrance finished eating, gathered his bow and quiver, and walked out of the armory door toward the stables. His horse in his stall was a beautiful golden steed Torrance had won in an archery contest about four years earlier. He named his prize Palmaro. He thought it was a clever play on words. After all, he is a Palomino; Torrance laughed as he thought back to the day he had named him. The Knight mounted the horse and was on his way. Torrance soon came to the spot where he and Orian agreed upon, and sure as the sun rose in the sky, there he was.

"Good morning, young knight," Orian said, smiling. "Good morning to you, Sir," Torrance resounded. "I trust you slept well?" the Wizard asked. "Yes, I did," the young man replied, not letting any hint of the visions that had overcome his dreams show. Torrance was anxious to start his training but tried not to seem too anxious. He asked, "When shall we start?" "Soon," Orian said, "but first, I have to teach you what I was trying to reveal to you in the dream." Torrance replied, "But you told me yesterday." "What I told you was not complete. I only told you what I thought you should know for now. There is much to learn. We are going to start at the beginning, and soon enough, you will come to know your full potential."

Torrance sat next to the Wizard and listened carefully to what he began to tell him. Orian began going over what he had told Torrance the day before, "Do you recall when I told you about your mother?" he asked. "Of course I do," the Knight replied, trying not to seem rude, "you only told me yesterday. Why would I not remember?" he asked. "There are unseen forces that may try to make our tasks harder," he replied. "I came to you in your dreams. What makes you think I am the only one that can get to you in that manner?" Torrance looked puzzled and unsettled. "Are there other wizards?" he asked nervously. "Yes, my boy," Orian said. "There are others. Some are trustworthy, but some would like to see harm come to you. I told you how Amiana put a spell on King Gavin. Did you think she just disappeared? I have felt her presence within the lands surrounding Plaitura since the dragons have not responded to my calls. Orian explained to Torrance the difference between wizards and sorceresses, "You must learn how to distinguish the two. Some wizards do not have good intentions, and not all sorceresses are evil," Orian said, then smiled and winked. "As they say, with time comes experience. I will guide you," Orian said with confidence, which made Torrance feel safe.

'We do not have much time, so let us begin," said the Wizard. "First, the dragons. As I told you, they each have special abilities. I will give you every detail you will need to know. These creatures are the hope of the kingdom and your destiny; they are linked." Torrance, still a little confused, listened intensely. Orian told the Knight to take his hand. Torrance complied and took hold of his hand; it felt like Orian had transported them to another place and time. This was true. They had been transported not to another time but to the top of a mountain. "On this mountain, the dragons live, so it is only logical that we shall start here. Do you agree?" Orian asked Torrance. "You are the teacher," he replied, "I trust you, and since you have the knowledge I need, we shall start here." A wise answer, Orian thought, I know I came at the right time. He is ready.

THE DRAGONS

Orian began, his voice soft and confident, "Torrance, you must remember all I have to tell you today." He nodded in agreement.

"First, the most powerful dragon is:

Nezaro the Fire Dragon: He is the oldest and most powerful of all. He can breathe fire and can fly higher than any other dragon. He is the leader. You will know him by his red color intertwined with golden specks. Nezaro is the leader of the clan. He will carry on the bloodline of the dragons.

Next is:

Ersella the Ice Dragon: She is next in line and is the younger sister of Nezaro. She is special in her ability to breathe ice. This has never been present in any dragon through the ages. Ersella is a white dragon with light blue wings with silver specks running through the blue. Her

ability is quite a remarkable sight. She can change the landscape into a winter splendor with one breath.
Third:

Myreil the Wind Dragon: Also white in color with tinges of lavender throughout her wings. Her ability is to control the direction of the wind. She can fly so fast that she seems to be almost invisible. Myreil is also a fire-breather, but with her unique talent, she can control the temperature of her breath."

With each description, Orian blew a puff of smoke from his pipe that looked like the dragon he spoke of to Torrance. The Knight watched. Torrance examined each vision mentally, noting their features, sizes, and colors. While he looked at the apparitions, they seemed to dance in the air and then fade. Torrance, trying to remember all that Orian had told him so far, looked up at the Wizard, then cocked his head and said, "I think I see the connection." Orian gazed at him. "What do you think it is?" he asked. Torrance stood up and proclaimed, "The dragons represent the elements." "They do represent the elements in some way. You are correct; there is much more you will learn," Orian replied. Orian thought, He will save Plaitura. He shall prevail.

Orian took hold of Torrance's hand again. Now, they sat under the tree where they had met this morning. Torrance looked at the wizard and asked, "Why are we here? I want to learn more." Orian looked at the sky that had now become dark and starlit. The day had given way to night, "King Gavin will be waiting for you, my boy." Torrance said, "I did not realize it had become so late. I should not have been gone so long. I have ignored my training and have no stag to show for my absence." Orian, with a wave of his hand, produced a large twelve-point stag draped over the Knight's horse. Torrance mounted his steed, nodded to Orian, and asked, "Tomorrow, Sir?" Orian simply smiled, and then Torrance knew.

Torrance raced through the hillside into the field that led to the stables. He could see a group of Knights and stable hands gathering. Sir Kieran, Sir Michael, and Sir Louis stood at the stable door. "Great

33

hunt," Sir Michael shouted. "Shall I bring it to the butcher?" asked Henry, the stable boy. "Thank you," Torrance replied, "I think it will make a fine addition to dinner." Henry took the stag from Palmaro's back while another stable hand, Albert, took the knight's horse for grooming.

The knights gathered around Torrance, shaking his hand and congratulating him on his conquest. King Gavin heard the murmurs coming from the stable and came to see what everyone was talking about. He saw the large twelve-point stag being carried away to the butcher and caught up with Torrance. "Nice catch, my boy," he uttered, patting Torrance on the back. "We shall have a feast tomorrow night. I can almost taste it now," the King laughed. "The head will make a wonderful addition to the trophy room," he added. Torrance agreed. "The stags were where you had said they would be, Your Majesty; by the stream is where I put my arrow into the stag. He gave me a bit of a fight," Torrance said. "I think patience was a help. I did not chase him in haste. Instead, I tracked him and waited. The stag finally dropped, and I claimed my prize." Torrance and the knights regaled the story of the hunt over dinner. With the evening ending, the knights continued to talk about the conquest of the day; everyone patted Torrance for such a great kill. Torrance, preoccupied with the visions Orian showed him, anxiously awaited the night's end. He wanted to learn more. Torrance studied the images in his mind repeatedly. King Gavin bid a good night to all as he left the dining area, then proceeded up the stairs to his bed chamber. One by one, the Knights left, and Torrance started to make his way to his quarters. Visions of dragons and Orian filled his mind as he lay in his bed and drifted off to sleep.

DAY THREE

Morning came, but not quickly enough for Torrance. Before the sun rose, he was awake, dressed, and ready to embrace the lessons of the day. On his way out of his quarters, he spotted Elaina walking down the corridor. "Good morning, Sir Torrance," she said. "Good morning to you!" he exclaimed, then took her by the arms and twirled Elaina around as if they were dancing. They both laughed. This has been the way they greeted each other since they were mere children playing in the great halls. Torrance and Elaina walked together down the stairs to the breakfast area, where she took her leave of him; she headed into the kitchen to start preparing the morning meal for the King and his knights.

Torrance was not the first up at this early time. As he walked into the room, he saw Sir Michael and Sir Kieran seated in their usual spots. "Good morning," he said as he took his seat. The knights were still talking about the size of the stag Torrance had brought back from his hunt.

Sir Michael said, "I think today we shall hunt for stags together, that is if you are planning to hunt this morning." Torrance fell silent for a moment, then replied, "I was thinking of going, but I did not want to press my luck any further. Besides, I have things to tend to before the feast tonight." Just then, King Gavin entered the room. The knights rose and bowed. "Good morning, Your Majesty," they chanted in unison. "Good morning, my good Knights," the King replied, "Please take your seats." Sir Louis followed behind; he made a stop at the blacksmith's station. "I am sorry, Your Majesty," he said as he took his spot, "I tried not to be late for the first meal." "That is alright," King Gavin said. "I just now arrived, and you are not late." The Knights sat down, and the servants brought in their morning meal. While they ate, the knights discussed their plans for the day. Sir Michael decided he and Sir Anthony would go hunting and try their luck by the stream. Sir Kieran would stay behind and train the squires; he is the sergeant-at-arms. King Gavin was pleased to see his knights together. He could remember when they were squires. Such anxious young lads, he thought, now they are Knights. King Gavin could trust his life to them, and they felt close to the King as well. Torrance, "What are your plans for this beautiful day?" the King asked. "I thought I would take a ride in the country, Sire," Torrance replied, "or I might go fishing. It would be a nice addition to the meal." "Fine, my boy," King Gavin said, "That sounds like a good idea. "Are you going to the stream?" he asked. "No, Your Majesty. I thought I might ride past the waterfall to the other side. If there are stags that big by the stream, I can only imagine the size of the fish on the other side of the falls. The underwater plant life is abundant there, so I would think the fish are quite nourished," Torrance laughed as he got up from the table to set out on his way.

Palmaro was ready to go as Torrance approached the stables. Albert had already fed, watered, and saddled him as per Torrance's orders. He mounted his steed and took off into the woods to the spot where Orian would be waiting. "Good Morning!" Orian shouted as he saw

Torrance arrive. "A very good morning indeed! I am anxious to know more," the Knight said as he dismounted his steed and tied him to a nearby branch. Orian once again took hold of Torrance's hand and transported them to the Dragon Mountain. They sat facing each other. The wizard lit his pipe and began, "I told you of the first three dragons; now you will learn about the last three dragons. They are:

"Solarid – The Sky Dragon: His color is midnight blue, straddled with silver throughout his wings. The silver then connects with the blue at the back of his neck and runs down to the tip of his tail. Solarid is also a fire-breather; his ability is unique. He controls the movements of the sun, moon, and stars.

Hedradon – The Earth Dragon: His body is green with brown wings. His ability is one we could not live without; his breath emanates a mist in the morning that gives nourishment to all the flora in the lands.

Armonius –The Harmony Dragon: She is the dragon of peace. Her colors are green with yellow on the underside of her wings, and the crest of her head is red. Armonius brings all the life together, creating a harmonious balance within the land. Her gift is that of a dragon song. When she sings, every creature in the land feels her inner peace.

I must know if you can recall all that I told you yesterday," Orian inquired. Torrance recited every detail of the past day. "Good!" Orian exclaimed. "I have to make sure no other has erased your teachings. Today, you will learn of the importance of the abilities these dragons possess. They are a crucial part of this world as we know it."

Orian explained that he had the pleasure of naming the dragons. As they hatched, he would watch them grow and present their abilities, and then Orian would give each one a name befitting them based on what they could do. Torrance was awestruck as the wizard talked. He had so many questions racing through his mind, yet none emerged from his lips. Orian continued, "All dragons are fire breathers; they know how to control it when they have to." Orian turned to

Torrance, patting him on the shoulder as if to say he would be all right. Then, he reached into his robe and took out a charm. Orian proclaimed, "I have something for you, Torrance." He put the charm into the knight's hand. "My boy," he said, "keep this with you always; it will protect you from the evil ones that might attempt to come into your dreams." The charm was a silver dragon head with eyes the color of the sun, and in the dragon's mouth was a single shard of crystal. Torrance accepted the wizard's gift with a smile, and he knew he would be safe. When Orian looked over at the young knight, he let out a sigh of relief. He thought he would do well. Torrance is a quick learner, and he is strong in body and mind. He will be King, Orian said, but only to himself; if I let him know how strong he is, he might start to get overconfident, then all would be lost.

Just as quickly as they had been transported to Dragon Mountain, they were back under the willow tree. The sun was beginning to fade, and Torrance knew he had to take his leave. "What was your excuse today?" Orian asked

Torrance. "I told everyone I was going fishing." Another wave of his hand, a string of fish appeared, strapped to Palmaro's saddle. "Thank you," the knight said as he rode out of sight. "I will be here tomorrow," he said as his voice trailed off.

Torrance gave the fish to Elaina, who was by the kitchen doorway when he arrived. "Will you take these to the cook for me?" he asked, "I have to change for the feast." Elaina took the fish from the knight's hand and replied, "I would be happy to." She turned toward him and gave him a grin. As Elaina walked into the kitchen, Torrance walked into the outer hallway to the great stairs that led to his quarters. He sat for a moment, then took the charm out of his pocket and stared at it. I hope you can protect me he said, looking at the charm. He changed for the feast, carefully choosing his outfit. He knew there would be many ladies waiting there, so he wanted to look his best. He walked into the grand ballroom, decorated with beautiful floral arrangements and filled with many people, most of whom Torrance knew.

King Gavin thought a buffet would be nice instead of a formal dinner, so the servants set tables along the south wall. Food was abundant; in the center of the main table was the stag Torrance had shot with the one that the other knights had bagged next to it. The fish were arranged nicely on a platter beside the stags. On every table, there were plates of fruits and vegetables and barrels of ale.

King Gavin, seated on his throne on the north side of the room, announced, "Let the festivities begin." Torrance joined his fellow Knights who were standing together and talking on the west side of the room. "Nice fish you caught today," Sir Michael said, "did you happen to see the stag Sir Anthony and I shot today?" he asked. "No, I did not," Torrance replied, "I arrived late and changed quickly. How big was it?" Sir Anthony replied, "It was an eight-pointer, not quite as big as yours was, but a fair catch, I would say." "Yes indeed. I would say so, too," Torrance proclaimed. During the evening, many of the King's court congratulated the knight on his great catch. The musicians started to play, the guests started to dance, and almost everyone at the feast was now paired and twirling around the ballroom as if they were dancing on clouds. Torrance and his friends were looking for dance partners when out of the center of the ballroom came a beautiful woman. They all vied for her attention, but her eyes were set on Torrance. She was a thin woman who had blonde hair, green eyes, and a petite figure. Torrance smiled at her and started to walk toward her to ask her to dance. Sir Michael cut him off and asked her first. As they began to dance, Torrance did not know if he should have been mad or glad for him as the couple danced by him. Torrance felt an uneasiness inside him. The charm in his pocket gave off an eerie warmness. The knight did his best to stay away from the woman. Every time she was near, the charm gave off the same sensation. He thought that Orian had given it to him at the right time. The feast was ending, and the guests were leaving, bidding good night to the King and his Knights. The woman who had given Torrance such an uneasy feeling had also left the feast.

Torrance bid all a good night and went to his quarters, glad the party was over. He tried to memorize every detail of the young woman's face. What was it about her that made him feel so leery of her? Is this the feeling of evil, or am I just nervous about all that Orian has told me?

As he lay in his bed, Torrance could not shake the feeling the woman emanated every time she was near him. "I have to let Orian know what happened tonight," he said aloud as if Orian could hear him. The knight clutched the charm tight in his hand and drifted off to sleep. He did not sleep long, though; the thoughts of the woman woke him, making him feel ill at ease. Torrance could not wait for the sunrise; he did not like the feelings this night brought to him, and, for the first time since he was a youngster, he feared the night.

Denise DeCarolis

DAY FOUR

At last, the sun arose. Torrance quickly dressed, left the castle, and rushed to the willow tree. Orian sensed his need to be early and was under the tree waiting. As Torrance explained what happened at the feast, Orian said, "Why do you think I am already here? I knew something was not right last night. I felt a presence, and it was quite disturbing. Torrance replied, "I was uneasy around this woman. Sir Michael danced with her, but her eyes were on me; the charm you gave me seemed to heat up whenever she came near. I could not wait for the feast to end." He continued, "After it was over, I went to my quarters and still could not shake the feeling this woman possessed." Orian said, "We must put her out of our minds for now. We have to hasten your lessons." "I did not think Amiana would be aware of our meetings so soon," the wizard said. "Do you think this woman is Amiana?" Torrance asked. "No, my boy. She does not have the ability to change her appearance. It must be another sorceress that is helping her," Orian said.

"Now, my boy, I will teach you how to contact the dragons. It is easy. All you have to do is picture one of them in your mind and call their name. If you are successful, you will see the dragon respond to you in your mind. It is almost as if you can see through their eyes. Now try it," Orian commanded Torrance. "All right, I will try," he said. Torrance tried to contact Nezaro, the fire dragon. He closed his eyes and concentrated. Something hit him like a bolt of lightning and threw him back against the tree. Torrance opened his eyes, and Orian looked at him with concern on his face. "What happened?" he asked. "I saw him," Torrance said. "He is magnificent. He looked into my mind, but there was something else. He is in pain, a pain so great that I could feel it, and there is a sadness surrounding him. We have to hurry, Orian. I do not think we have much time," the knight insisted. Orian agreed. He took hold of the knight's hand, and they were once again on top of Dragon Mountain.

Orian lit a small fire. He took a pouch out of his robe; the wizard poured the contents of the pouch into his hand. It looked like red clay powder in his hand; he put his hand near the flame and slowly poured the dust into it. The flame began to rise, and an image began to appear. It started to take the form of a dragon. As quickly as it appeared, the image shattered, and the flame died out. Orian, taken aback, exclaimed, "That has never happened; the evil must be more powerful than I could have anticipated. We must make haste." "How do we conquer this evil, Orian? The power seems to me to be greater than your magic," Torrance said, not trying to sound condescending towards the wizard. "Do not doubt my magic, boy," Orian said sternly. "I have many secrets that can help you, but you have to believe in me." Torrance apologized to the wizard, and with that statement, they were once again under the willow tree. "You must go to King Gavin and ask if it would be possible for you to take leave for a while," Orian said. "What would I say would be the reason for my leave, Orian?" Torrance continued, "How should I answer any questions the King would ask me about my leave?" Orian replied, "You'll know, my boy. You'll know."

Torrance raced Palmaro back to the castle. He dismounted, handed his horse to Albert, and entered the courtyard to the castle stairs. As he climbed the stairs, he met Elaina. He asked, "What room is his Highness in?" She replied, "His Majesty is in the sitting room." "Is he alone or with court business?" the knight asked. "King Gavin is alone now and not involved with any pressing matters," Elaina said. "Thank you," the knight said as he started down the long hallway toward the King's sitting room. As he approached the door, his heart raced. How do I ask for a leave? What reason should I give? he thought. Torrance knocked on the sitting room door. "Enter," the voice said from inside. He made his way through the doorway into the room where King Gavin was seated. The knight started to speak when he was interrupted by the King. "Torrance, my son," he said, "I have a matter that needs to be addressed in the South, and I think it would be good training for you to go in my stead. It is an easy task, but it will take you a few days to complete," the King stated. "There is a land to the South, and the people need assistance with their land. You are to go with supplies from our people to help; it seems that something has poisoned their crops. You will take what you can and go to Scandos. King Rufus is an old friend, and I shall not turn my back on him in his time of need." Torrance bowed to King Gavin and accepted the task willingly. "This will help our relationship with Scandos, and I think it is about time you see the lands around you. You will meet new people and possibly make new friendships along the way."

The Knight retired to his quarters to prepare for the journey. As he slept, he dreamt of the dragon that he saw in his vision. He saw the fire dragon standing on a mountain with shackles holding him down. The dream faded from his mind. It was now morning, the time to take on the task the king had set before him.

Denise DeCarolis

DAY FIVE

Torrance entered the breakfast room before any of the other Knights. He ate a quick meal and set out for the stables. Albert was also awake early to help prepare for the trip. He stocked Palmaro's saddlebags full, and alongside Torrance's steed stood another horse used just for supplies. King Gavin came to the stables to bid the knight a safe and successful trip. "Good luck, my boy. Be safe," the King said. "Thank you, Your Majesty," he responded, "I will do my best to help in any way I can." "I know you will, Torrance. You have the best teacher," the King laughed.

Palmaro took off at full gallop. "Safe journey," King Gavin said as the knight departed. Torrance waved in recognition. As he rode off on his journey, he could not help thinking that Orian had something to do with the circumstances surrounding the king's decision to send him on this mission. Torrance came to the willow tree where he knew Orian would be waiting.

51

"Good morning, young knight," Orian said as Torrance dismounted his steed. "You would not have a hand in the King's sending me to Scandos, would you now?" Torrance asked. The Wizard answered, "Maybe I did, and maybe I did not; how do you know it was not fate? You have many things to do on this trip, but I will be with you to guide you through the tough times." Orian and Torrance prepared to mount up, but before they got on their horses, the wizard gave Torrance a quick and very important lesson. He taught him how to use the charm to keep the evil ones from seeing into his thoughts and dreams. He gave Torrance a chain to put the charm on. It was also silver, but Orian sprinkled it with magic powder, explaining that this powder contained dragon's blood. Orian said, "This is one of the more potent ingredients in my possession. It will strengthen the charm's magic." Orian told him to say to himself before he went to sleep, "Let no one come into my dreams or interrupt my sleep." (But only Orian knew the Knight did not have to speak a word; the charm and chain would protect him. He told him to say these words to make him feel like he had a part in the magic.)

Torrance thanked the wizard. "I trust you; I know it will protect me. I can feel the power already." The men mounted their steeds and rode off toward Scandos. The trip to Scandos would take at least two days, so the knight and the wizard would have time to prepare for the task ahead. As they rode, they talked about the dragons and Amiana. Orian told Torrance about his family history and how this would affect the outcome of their journey.

Torrance had almost forgotten that his mother would be at the castle in Scandos. "Will I know her when I see her? Will she know me?" he asked Orian. Orian replied, "Do you actually think a mother would forget her own son?" "It has been twelve long years since last we were together," Torrance said. "I am certain I do not look the same," he laughed. Orian told him he had contacted Lenore before he came to him in the dream, and she knew she would see her son once again. "She told me not a single day went by that she did not think of you, Torrance. Her only concern was that you would have forgotten her by now." "Why would my mother think I would have ever forgotten her?" "She, too, knows of the evil that has come over the lands and into dreams," Orian said. "Your mother is worried," the wizard continued, "She knows what is in front of you, and she could not bear to lose another."

As they rode on, the landscape seemed to take on a darkness Torrance had never seen. He noticed trees with leaves that had crumbled and turned different shades other than what they were supposed to be for this time of the season. The flowers were wilting, and the grass was brown.

Torrance and Orian looked around in dismay. "Is this connected to the dragons' disappearance?" Torrance asked. Orian replied, "Yes, my knight, now you see why we must make haste. The longer the dragons are bound to Amiana, the harder it will be to get them back. All the lands and everything you have come to know will fade from sight. Plaitura will become barren, without crops or water to feed and nourish the people, and soon, every other land will follow. The good will perish, and Amiana will succeed," Orian said. "I will not let that happen," Torrance announced with a newfound confidence.

"Night is falling. We should find a spot to rest; the horses need food and water, and we could do with rest as well," Orian said. After the horses were watered and fed, Orian created a meal for the knight and himself. As they sat and ate, the wizard taught Torrance some helpful tricks. He taught him how to use leaves to guide him. "They will bend in the direction you need to go if you should ever lose your way," Orian said. "It is getting late, and we shall need an early start. We have a long way to go," the wizard said as he lay next to the fire. Torrance agreed and laid down. He held the charm tight in his hand as he fell asleep. Orian did not sleep, though. He kept a watchful eye on the knight as he slept.

DAY SIX

When Torrance awoke, he found Orian awake, smoking his pipe as usual. He sat up. "Good morning, Orian," he said without a response. The knight repeated, "Good morning." Orian looked at the knight. He then spoke in an alarming tone. "Is it?" he said. "Look around, my boy." Although he knew it was morning, when Torrance finally stood up and looked around, what he saw made his heart feel heavy. It was not quite dark as night, but the land looked dismal. All the flowers and trees were dead, the animals were gone, and there were no songs from birds or chirping from the morning locusts. "What has happened here?" Orian replied, "This happened overnight; I watched as everything in this place died, yet I could not do anything. Without the dragons, everything that exists will wither and eventually die! We must go," Orian said. "Quickly, Torrance, mount your steed; we must ride like the wind! The knight complied. He mounted his steed, and the two rode off.

Orian spoke softly from aboard his horse, so softly that Torrance could not make out what he was saying. The knight knew what Orian was doing. He was trying to undo the wickedness that had overcome the land. Torrance dared not interrupt him, for he knew if he did, he would break his concentration. When the wizard had finished, he turned to Torrance and said, "I tried, Torrance, but I seem to have no effect without the dragons. I feel useless." "You are not useless," Torrance responded. "Without you, I would not have known my true identity, and we would not be here today." He tried to make the wizard realize that he is important because without him, everything would be lost. "I know we will be victorious in my heart," the young knight said with confidence. Orian smiled as he listened to the words Torrance spoke. He thought, I believe in you, my boy! The two rode as fast as the horses could go, but they knew it would not reach Scandos by the day's end. They looked for a place to rest for the night; they needed shelter since the weather grew cold and rainy. Torrance found a spot near the lake's edge. It was under a bluff and provided enough shelter for the two. Orian made a fire as the knight fished. He caught enough fish for the two to be full and energized for the next day's ride. After they finished eating, they watered and fed the horses and then made makeshift beds out of leaves and moss. Orian continued to teach Torrance things he would need to reclaim the dragons. "They need to be familiar with your scent and your face," the wizard said. "Dragons are remarkable creatures," Orian told Torrance. "You will be surprised when you finally see them for yourself." The knight imagined himself standing amid the dragons as he fell asleep. Orian took his usual spot, watching over Torrance while he slept. He knew he dared not sleep, for then he would be putting them both in danger. He could protect them from unseen forces with his magic. He knew if he slept, those forces would try to stop Torrance through his dreams.

DAY SEVEN

As they rode towards Scandos, they saw that the land was almost barren of foliage. Torrance thought, I cannot believe what I am seeing. It is worse than I imagined. Orian saw the look on the young knight's face. "I can see you did not expect to see this much damage in one place." "No," replied the knight sullenly, shaking his head in disbelief.

As they approached the outer gate of Scandos, some people from the village started to gather around them. King Rufus waited on the castle stairs until they were closer; he then greeted the two with a smile of relief on his face. "Welcome," King Rufus said and continued with a distraught tone in his voice, "to what is left of my Kingdom." "Your Majesty, it is an honor to make your acquaintance," Torrance said, bowing before the king. "I am sorry it could not have been under different circumstances," he said to the king apologetically. "I hope we can help your kingdom and your people, Your

Highness." King Rufus replied, "I could see a great relief on the faces of my people the moment the two of you arrived." Torrance dismounted his steed and began passing out the supplies King Gavin had sent with him. The people of Scandos unloaded the horses with a cheerfulness that had not been seen in the Kingdom for some time. Torrance felt something he had not felt in a long time. It was a loving glance; he looked around and found a woman looking at him, smiling. It looked almost like a sad smile. He knew this woman's face, the face of his mother. She was smiling down at him from the castle stairs. He continued to unload the supplies. When his work was done, he ran up the stairs into the arms of his mother.

"Torrance, my son," Lenore cried, "it has been such a long time. I did not think this day would come." "Nor I, mother," Torrance replied as he held back his tears. "I did not want to leave you, my son, but I could not stay in Plaitura any longer, and I knew the King would take proper care of you." The knight took his mother in his arms and whispered, "It is alright, Mother; Orian told me everything. I knew someday we would see each other again." He continued, speaking in whispers, "I have dreamt of this day." Lenore responded, "As I have to my son." With the hardest part of their reunion out of the way, they continued to help the villagers and the rest of the Kingdom with the unloading of the cargo.

King Rufus was grateful for the help King Gavin had sent him. After they were finished, they all went into the castle and continued talking and planning for the days ahead. King Rufus had his cooks prepare what little food they had for their guests. Orian and Torrance thanked the King for his graciousness; they then started planning for the rest of their journey. The evil that plagued them would not stop, even though the castle walls seemed sturdy enough for Torrance until Orian reminded him that even sturdy walls could not keep evil out. As the night ended, the king showed his guests to their quarters. They talked about the replenishing of the kingdom. As they reached the quarters, King Rufus bid Torrance and Orian a good night. Lenore kissed her son gently on the cheek and said, "Sleep well, my son, for there is much to do." "Good night, Mother," Torrance said as he kissed her goodnight. In their chambers, Orian and Torrance talked almost half the night away. Orian spoke about all that Torrance would face in the days to come. He told him something he never had expected.

"Torrance, my boy, I have hidden a secret from you," the wizard said as he gazed out the window at the land. "What have you not told me, old man?" Torrance said sharply. Orian looked at the knight and said, "It is about your mother." "Tell me!" Torrance demanded. "I was trying to find the proper words but have yet to find them," Orian said, "I have no choice but to come right out with the truth. Your mother has powers also," he said with a sigh of relief. There, I said it, he thought as he looked at the Knight. Torrance had a look on his face as if he did not hear the words. Orian opened his mouth and started to repeat himself but was quickly interrupted by the knight. "You did not need to tell me," he said. "I felt it when she held me." "Now I know why I am the one for this task," he continued. "When my mother took me in her arms, I felt her power, and I also saw visions. I could not make them out clearly, though." Orian asked, "Why did you not tell me? I was trying all day to figure out ways to tell you about your mother. You could have made it easier for me," Orian laughed. Torrance said, "It was fun to watch you squirm," he said, toying with the wizard. "Besides, I was going to tell you tonight," the knight said as he laid down and fell asleep. Orian also fell asleep, for he knew they were safe here for now. Orian and Torrance slept uninterrupted until sunrise, when a beam of sunlight came through the window. The beam was so bright that the knight almost forgot where he was. The sun was warm on his face; Torrance stretched and bid Orian a good morning. Orian had slept better than he had in several days and awoke refreshed and ready to face the day.

Denise DeCarolis

DAY EIGHT

Torrance and Orian dressed and went to the King's private chambers, where Lenore joined them. They laid out the plans to replenish the land, and they would gather the people together to get started. After the discussion, Orian, Torrance, and Lenore walked through the fields, informing the people of the hard work that lay ahead. Torrance told the people of Scandos, "There is much work to be done. If you all pull together, it can be done." The people agreed and quickly started to work in the fields, tilling soil and replanting seeds. Smiling, Torrance looked at Orian and said, "It looks like they will be all right. They seem to enjoy the work." The wizard replied, "When stomachs are empty, the weak prevail, my boy."

Torrance and his mother walked away from the fields to a clearing in the woods. There, they came upon a place to sit. Lenore told her son how sorry she was to have left him. She told him everything he needed to know about her powers. At first, he looked confused. If my own mother is a sorceress, what does that make me? he wondered. His thoughts then turned to Amiana and how she used her powers to bewitch King Gavin. Did my mother do the same to King Artis? Lenore knew what her son was thinking. "No!" his mother screamed. She turned to her son with tears welling in her eyes. I never used my magic on your Father; we loved each other truly and unconditionally. When we met, I was unaware of my powers," his mother insisted. "I was merely a child. As with you and Elaina, I grew up with King Artis. We played together and shared many secrets, and when we were older, we came to a point in our lives when we knew we were meant to be together. Your father was a good man, honest, caring, and loving. He loved you, too, and every smile you gave him went straight to his heart. I did not want him to enter that tournament. He would always trust my feelings, but for some reason, he did not heed my warning and took the challenge. They say you cannot change destiny. Well, whoever said it was right!" Torrance's mother had a solemn look on her face as she walked slowly back towards the courtyard. He knew then that her decision to leave Plaitura was the right one. Her heart was still in pain just by the memory of that fateful day when his father had lost his life. Torrance followed his mother, staying a step behind; he did not want her to see the look on his face as he thought of what might happen to him and the lands if he did not succeed in freeing the dragons and defeating the evil that held them. Before he let Lenore out of his sight, he grabbed her hands, gave them a gentle kiss, and whispered, "I will succeed, Mother." Lenore walked to the courtyard stairs and watched as her son prepared to leave.

Orian waited for him at the castle of King Rufus. "Torrance, my boy, we do not have much time. We must take our leave," the wizard said. The horses were saddled and packed with supplies, waiting to go. Torrance looked back at the fields. I think they will be just fine, he said to himself as he approached Orian. A stable boy handed the knight his reins, bid him a safe journey, and thanked them for coming to the aid of their land. King

Rufus thanked the wizard and Torrance for helping his people to overcome such hard times. Lenore, standing by King Rufus' side, just smiled and waved goodbye.

DAY NINE

Orian was adamant about getting to Zebulon as quickly as possible. The days were growing darker. Zebulon is the name of the Dragon's Mountain, which is where they would have to go to free the dragons under Amiana's control. When Orian had taken Torrance there, it was only an apparition, not the real mountain. He wanted to show the Knights where they would be facing their challenge. Torrance already felt like he knew every inch of Zebulon even though he had only been there in an apparition. Now, he was anxious to get there and face his challenge. "Hurry up, old man," the knight called to Orian, who was lagging on his horse. "Do not worry, my young friend. We will get there soon enough." With a slight kick to the side of his horse, Orian caught up to the knight. Now, side-by-side, Orian could instruct Torrance while they rode. "You know it will not be easy to climb the mountain," he said. "It is half a day's journey to the lowest point where we can rest," he continued. "I thought we could get there by your magic," Torrance said. "No, we cannot use magic to climb Zebulon!" Orian exclaimed. "This will make you stronger, and when you finally face whatever forces are holding the dragons, your strength will help you become victorious!"

Torrance, now more determined than ever to get to Zebulon, rode Palmaro harder. "Easy, boy. We still have far to go, and you do not want to lose your prize steed, do you now?" The knight slowed his pace; he remembered what Orian had said to him about patience. Torrance fell silent for a while. His thoughts raced in his mind, and then he finally spoke, "Orian, what if I do not succeed? What if Amiana is too strong?" "The first thing you must do, my boy, is put those thoughts out of your mind. A sorceress or wizard can sense your self-doubt and control you," Orian told him. "They will prey on your fears and weakness, and the outcome would be catastrophic." They continued to ride toward Dragon Mountain, but at a slower pace, for the night was beginning to fall, and they had to find shelter for themselves and the horses. They came to a clearing slightly off the path they were traveling in the neighboring land of Iverson. There, they found a stream where they could get fresh water, and they hunted for food, built a fire, and settled in for the evening. The two talked about their time in Scandos, watching all the people come together to help rebuild their land. Orian asked Torrance what he felt when he saw his mother for the first time after so many years. He replied, "It was as if we were never apart. There is such a strong bond between us." He paused for a moment, looked Orian in the eyes, and said, "That is something that will never fade." The wizard just smiled, lit his pipe, and said, "You have grown, son. You have grown."

The darkness fell around them, then the stars faded, and the clouds rolled in. As it began to rain, the storm seemed to make everything around them take on an eerie feeling. A strange chill in the air made Orian uneasy. Torrance felt it, too. The knight sat up and looked around. He felt as if something or someone was watching them. He started to speak, but Orian stopped him with a gesture and whispered, "Do not say a word, my boy. There is something out there!" A cold wind blew past the two, and as quick as it came, it was gone! "I fear there are more involved than I had thought," Orian said, almost as if he was contemplating who it could be. "I thought for sure Amiana was the only one who could do such things as to imprison my dragons!"

Torrance sat silent for a moment, thoughts racing through his mind, "Orian, how do we know what powers the others will possess? What I mean to say is, do you know every wizard and sorceress in the land?" Orian replied, "I know most of them, or so I think. There seem to be different powers I am feeling now." Orian and Torrance sat up most of the night for fear that someone or something would try to harm them as they slept. Torrance remembered that Orian told him someone could come into his dreams as the wizard had done to contact him. Torrance felt lucky that Orian had come to him first. If the others would have gotten to him before Orian, there is no telling what the outcome would be! They had to just get through this night, for Zebulon was not far, and their focus was to free the dragons and banish the evil that was holding them captive.

The sun was beginning to rise. Torrance felt a sense of relief as it became lighter, and the day did not seem as ominous as the night. Orian filled the water jugs and started to load up the horses when he heard a noise behind him. There, in the shadows of a large tree, was a figure he thought he recognized. He moved closer, only to find himself caught in a trap. The knight knew Orian would not take this long to fetch water for the journey; he knew something was wrong. He ran to the stream and then turned and saw the wizard standing strangely still near a tree. He called him, but he did not get a response. He tried a second time, but still nothing. He ran to the wizard's side, putting his hand on his shoulder, but there was no movement! The knight started to panic. What should I do? Think, he said to himself. Do not just stand here. He is in trouble. His mind seemed to be having an inner conflict with itself. Then, like a bolt of lightning hit him, he knew what to do. He took the pendant out of his pocket, held it up in front of the wizard, and began to chant. He did not know where the words were coming from, but he knew they were the right words. His voice became louder and the words stronger, and then suddenly, Orian snapped out of his malaise. "What happened?" he asked the knight. Torrance replied, "You were under a spell of some kind." "Then what brought me out of it?" he asked. "I did," Torrance proclaimed with a new-found confidence. "I did not know what to do at first," he said, "but then it came to me as if I had always known what to do. I used the pendant. Words came out of my mouth that I have never spoken, and now you are all right." "My boy, you are the chosen one. No one would have known the words to break the spell that held me." "Orian," Torrance said, "I heard my mother's voice speaking the very same words that I spoke to break the spell that bound you!" Orian said, "It does not matter, my boy. You still knew what to do and how to save me, and I am forever in your debt, my boy. Now, we must make haste, for we do not have much time. Zebulon is a half-day ride from here. We should saddle up and go."

DAY TEN

The horses' hooves made a thunderous sound as Orian and Torrance raced toward Zebulon. The knight was very anxious to reach their destination. As they rode, he saw the peak of the mountain coming into view. A chill of excitement ran through his body. He slowed his pace; for now, he could see the mountain and knew they would be there soon. Orian slowed his pace to keep up with the young knight. "This is the difficult part of the path we are about to come to," Orian said. "There are many narrow and winding trails ahead. Be cautious in these parts. Palmaro is a very special horse to you, and I would not want anything to happen to him or you," Orian said as they approached the base of the Dragon Mountain.

Torrance paused for a minute as he looked up at the path to the first clearing where they would have to rest for the night. It was a very steep and narrow path, but he was certain that they would be able to make it! Torrance

75

looked at the wizard and then his horse and said, "There is no time like the present, as they say, so we should go now." With that said, he tapped his horse with his heels and grabbed the reins tightly, then started his ascent slowly and carefully up the path to Zebulon. Orian followed closely, matching his horse's footing with that of Palmaro's. The journey up the mountain was slow, but still, they were making great strides. Orian was right. It would take at least a half-day to reach the first plateau. There was one spot where Torrance had misjudged the clearing, and his horse lost his footing and almost sent the two careening down the path. The knight quickly tightened the reins and pulled his horse to the left, regaining its balance. Orian called to him, "Are you all right?" Torrance replied, "Yes, we are, but make sure you do not make the same mistake; stay to the left." Orian took the advice of his junior and kept his horse to the left of the path.

Orian had made this journey hundreds of times but never on horseback. It was always on foot or dragon; he did not realize how treacherous it was. He was happy that Torrance was such a skillful horseman. The sun was setting, and the trail grew darker. The two seemed to be crawling inch by inch now. Finally, they had made the first plateau where they could rest for the night.

Orian dismounted his horse, as did Torrance. "Slow ride, but we made it," he said with a sigh of relief in his voice. Orian tied up the horses and began preparing a fire. As the sun set, the climate turned bitterly cold. Torrance's hands were raw from holding the reins so tightly, and now the cold was bothering them. He rubbed his hands together over the fire, which was now ablaze. Orian took a cup and warmed ale for the cold and weary travelers. Torrance took a sip and smiled. "You thought of all the right things to bring on this journey, my friend." "You must not have too much to drink, as tomorrow will bring one of the hardest tasks you will face." "I know. I can feel the dragon's anguish; they are being held against their will. I can sense they want to be freed," Torrance said sadly.

Orian had more instructions for the knight. He told him of new spells and chants that he would need to defeat the ones that held his dragons. "They know we are here," Orian said. "They have tracked every step of our journey." Torrance looked at the wizard, who seemed to have aged just a little since they had started out on their quest. He replied, "I have known all along." "During this trip, I have felt them watching us and waiting." "One thing I do not know, Orian, is why have they not come after me. Instead, they tried to take you out of the way," Torrance asked. "First of all, you possess the dragon amulet, and if you had not noticed, I have not slept much since we have been on this trip. I have been casting spells for protection over you every night, and by doing so, it had left me in a weakened state. It was easier for them to cast a spell over me in that condition than to try to get to you. I am sure they felt the power of the amulet you possess that, combined with my magic, made you safe." Torrance took hold of the wizard's shoulder and said, "I shall be forever in your debt for all you have done for me. Thank you, Orian."

Orian told Torrance to try to get some rest, for he would need every bit of strength he could muster. Torrance agreed and tried to rest but was anxious to save the dragons and felt as if he could not wait any longer. He then remembered what Orian had said when they had first met about having patience. The knight took a deep breath, looked up at the sky, and tried to relax. Then, all his thoughts seemed to run together. All the spells Orian had taught him, and every detail about each dragon were racing in his mind. He began to wonder if he would remember the right words to say when the time came. He wondered if his sword would be strong enough to break the chains that bound the dragons. Torrance just wanted to do the right thing and free the dragons so balance would return to the lands, but could he? The knight closed his eyes and started to drift into a peaceful slumber. He knew Orian would still be awake, watching over him and making sure nothing would harm him. With the confidence he had in Orian, Torrance fell asleep.

DAY ELEVEN

Torrance awoke to find Orian still awake, watching over him. It was still dark, even though he felt as if he had slept a full night's sleep. Indeed, he had. It was daybreak, and the weather was changing. It was dark and stormy, then the darkness gave way to sunlight and was changing every minute. "Orian, what is happening?" the knight asked. There was no answer for a moment, then Orian said, "It is Armonius. Because she was in torment, the weather would be unstable." With each change, Orian seemed to feel the pain of his beloved dragon. Torrance sat helpless, knowing that there was nothing he could do to comfort the wizard or ease his pain.

Now more than ever, Torrance felt he was ready to face his destiny. The sheer look of pain on the wizard's face made the knight more determined to take on the evil ones that held the precious dragons captive! Almost as quickly as it had started, it was over. The sun was shining brightly, and Orian was himself again. Torrance was glad to see Orian out of anguish and regaining his composure. "Why did it stop?" asked Torrance. "My dragon seems to be out of danger for the moment," replied the wizard. "I only hope she will be able to fend off any more attacks until we reach her. If she cannot, the trip will be harder on us." Torrance was ready to go, with his horse's reins in hand, waiting for Orian to mount his horse. Orian did not, though. He remained seated and motioned for the knight to sit beside him. "I know you have something on your mind, my boy, so now is the time to get it out." Torrance spoke to Orian in a soft voice, "You did not explain why there was no indication of anything in the land that was amiss," he continued, "Everyone in Plaitura was happy and healthy, the crops were plentiful, and there was not a thing out of the ordinary there." He paused as if he were trying to collect his thoughts and chose his words carefully. "How come no one noticed anything awry, including me, until we left Plaitura?" Orian looked Torrance in the eyes and replied, "We had to protect you, my young knight." "Who, besides

Denise DeCarolis

you, was protecting me?" "Your mother, of course!" Orian responded. "No one in Plaitura could know anything was out of the ordinary, and we made it so. It is just easier this way. No one feels the pain of the dragons, and the land and people of Plaitura do not suffer, as did the people of Scandos. Torrance asked, "Now that we have not been in Plaitura for some time, are the people still protected?" "Yes," Orian said with a smile on his face and a nod of his head. "I would be devastated if anything should happen to King Gavin," Torrance said.

Orian replied, "I would never let any harm come to your homeland or the people. I must inform you, though. We are protecting them now, but when you are fighting for the dragons, your mother and I will be using our magic to protect you. It might not be strong enough to continue protecting Plaitura for the duration of the battle," Orian continued, "but they will be so concentrated on you that I am sure Plaitura will be unharmed." "I only hope you are right, Orian. The people there are my family."

Torrance took some time for himself. Overlooking the land from the plateau, he stood alone. Orian let him be since he knew he had a lot to contemplate. The knight needed a clear head to prepare for tomorrow. Although Torrance knew he should be thinking about what he would have to do to free the dragons, he could not concentrate. All the thoughts that ran through his head were of his childhood, when he was in a happier place, playing with Elaina and starting his training with Sir Michael, Sir Kieran, and Sir Anthony and the quaint little breakfast room where they would just sit and talk. How he longed for those days to return, but he knew when the task was over, nothing would be the same! Torrance continued to stare out over the land, watching the sky as the changes were starting again. He could hear Armonius roaring in pain, and his heart sank. The sky grew dim, dark clouds covered the mountain, and it began to rain.

Orian called to the knight, "Torrance, come and sit by the fire. It is growing colder, and you need to eat." "I have no need for food right now," the knight replied. "I will, however, sit by the fire. As always, you are right, my friend. It is turning colder." Orian knew Torrance had many things going on in his mind, so he did not press the need for food with him. The night came quickly, and Torrance knew he needed to be at his best for the morning. He laid his head down and closed his eyes, but sleep did not come easy. The fire warmed him, and he tried to relax but was anxious for the morning to awaken. Throughout the night, Torrance went over different strategies for setting the dragons free, but he finally gave up, telling himself that whatever happened, everything would come together, and the dragons would be free once again. He knew Orian and his mother would help in any way possible, but the rest was up to him. He had to be strong and confident and just trust his instincts to know what to do. That did not seem to be enough to comfort him, though. He had the medallion and all the spells Orian had taught him, but he still had an uneasy feeling inside him.

The sun was rising. Torrance did not sleep at all, and Orian was still watching over him, smoking his pipe. The dawn held new concerns for Torrance. He found himself second-guessing his decision to take on the challenge that had been set before him. The knight continued to dress for the battle, knowing that he had to put those thoughts aside and proceed for the sake of the dragons and his people!

DAY TWELVE

Orian sensed Torrence's hesitation and spoke softly to him. "My boy, you know you can do this," he said. "After all, I have taught you everything you need to know to be victorious." Torrance looked at the wizard and sighed, "That is a great comfort to me, and I thank you for all you have done for me. Especially seeing my mother after all these years, I shall never forget your kindness." "Why do you speak as though you are not coming back, my young knight? I have every confidence in you, and I know you shall come back the victor!"

Torrance laughed at the wizard. Orian looked confused, "Have I said something to amuse you?" he asked. "No, you have not." Torrance could not stop the laughter emerging from his lips. "Then what is it that you find so amusing?" Orian asked. Torrance replied, "The look you get on your face. Your nose wrinkles in a curious kind of way, and your nostrils flare." "So, you find my face amusing, do you? You are not so handsome yourself!" Orian said with a jovial tone in his voice. The two started laughing and then hugged. Orian patted Torrance on his back. "I think we needed some relief from the pressure we are under," he said. "I agree," Torrance said. "That made me feel a little less ill at ease. I shall go ready myself."

The two started their ascent to the peak of Zebulon. The path was narrow, just wide enough for the horses. One false step or loss of footing would bring an untimely demise for the travelers. As they made their way up the path, they did not speak, for all their concentration was on the path. Lightning flashed all around them, but Torrance did not let that distract him from his task. The pace was slow and steady. Orian carefully watched the knight's horse's footing to steer his horse almost in the exact footprints, trying not to make any mistakes. Torrance spotted a clearing just below the peak and motioned to Orian to stop there. The wizard nodded. The ascent was taking longer than Torrance anticipated. He had wanted to get to the clearing to search his surroundings to figure out his plan for the attack. He needed to see what side he should climb, where the dragons were, and how many foes he would have to face. He knew that someone had been watching them for some time now, but how much they knew about the knight, he could only imagine. Now more than ever, he wondered if he should have told someone like Sir Michael or Sir Kieran. He would have felt more confident with them by his side.

Torrance also knew that it would be thoughts like those that would defeat him. He had to do this alone and not question his ability to rise to the occasion. Now, at the clearing, he dismounted his steed and started to plan his strategy. The lightning strikes seemed to be getting closer as Torrance started to look for a way to get to the peak. He could hear the sounds of the dragons and people talking. He needed to see how many he had to face to free the dragons. Orian called to him, "Come, let us try to figure this out together." The knight complied and sat beside the wizard. Using his staff, Orian started drawing up plans of attack in the dirt where they were sitting. Torrance remembered Orian telling him when they first met that he only had a fortnight to rescue the dragons, and time was short now. He put on his armor and listened to Orian's plan of attack. "If I go that way, I will be in direct sight of all who are holding the dragons," Torrance reminded the wizard. "Yes, that is the plan," Orian said, "For if you take your stance in plain sight, it will catch them off guard. They will be stumped for the moment." "I see what you are saying. They will not know how to react, and I will have the first-hand advantage." "Yes, my boy, now ready yourself."

Torrance made his way to the peak of Dragon Mountain. What he saw there made his heart sink. He remembered the visions of each dragon as Orian described them. When he saw them, their color had faded. Instead of the beautiful colors he was shown, they were now almost a brownish color. The knight could not tell one from the other. For a second, he stood frozen, not knowing what to do. Then he saw something that took him aback.

Bound to a tree, there he was. But who was it? Orian. It was the wizard, but how could that be? He had just left him below in the clearing. Torrance became confused and did not know what to do. His eyes raced around his surroundings, and then he came upon another startling sight: his mother bound next to Orian. Both seemed frozen in place. No emotions appeared on their faces, and not a single word emerged from their lips. He thought, How long were they held captive there? Who was guiding him to this place? Laughter resounded all around him. Then, an eerie sound came from beyond the trees, a deep thunderous voice. A figure stepped out from the darkness, another wizard who seemed to resemble Orian. Torrance took a step towards the figure that was as far as he had gotten. As he took his step, the wizard threw out his hand and spoke a word that shot the knight back. He landed on the ground, dazed for a moment; he tried to get to his feet. It took some doing, but after a second or so, Torrance got up and tried to move closer to the imposter. The knight took hold of his charm and chanted the words that Orian had told him to use, but they had no effect. That is when Torrance realized Orian had not been with him for some time. This imposter had brought him here. Torrance spoke. "Who are you? What have you done to my mother and Orian?" he shouted. The laugh returned, but no answer. "Who are you? Show yourself!" Torrance insisted. Still, no one came to answer to the knight's demands. All he could hear was the evil laugh taunting him.

The dragon's roars were now turning to whimpers. Torrance did not know what to do; his mind had gone blank. He wanted to run, but his feet stood steadfast. None of his training could have prepared him for what he was about to face. He then thought if he was to run, he would most probably have doomed the land. Again, he tried to coax out the imposter who had brought him to this point in time. "Why are you so afraid to show yourself?" Torrance shouted. "I know why you do not come to face me," he continued. "It is because you know you will be defeated!" This time, the knight received the response he was searching for the wizard imposter who came from beyond the trees to face him. Now, he looked nothing like Orian. He was older, and there was much more harshness to his features. Torrance could tell he was not a kindhearted person as Orian. How could he have deceived me? The knight wondered. "You know me, but I do not have the pleasure of your acquaintance," Torrance said to the figure now before him. "I am Morax," the man exclaimed as if Torrance should have known who he was. "I am the oldest and most powerful of all wizards." He moved slowly around the knight. "Orian is no match for me, and neither shall you be," the wizard proclaimed. Torrance thought Morax was right. He was no match for him, but then why would he bring him here if there were not a chance to succeed?

Torrance knew if he had wanted to kill him, he could have done that at any time. Why did he let me live? The knight pondered. He is toying with me. A voice rang in the knight's head, "You will be victorious. This is what you were trained for, my boy!" The voice was Orian's. In his frozen state, he was able to communicate with Torrance. The knight felt a sense of relief at that moment, and a smile came to his lips.

Morax looked at Torrance and then gazed behind him. The knight turned to see the woman who had made him feel so uneasy at the King's feast. "I am sure you remember meeting this sorceress. Her name is Fyndell. I thought she would have stopped you from coming this far," Morax confessed. "Luck must have been with you the night of the feast, for she has never disappointed me." Torrance looked at the woman who stood before him; he wondered how strong her powers were and how to approach the two that confronted him now.

Torrance's thoughts then turned to Orian and his mother bound to the tree. How could he free them? Once again, he heard the familiar voice of the wizard Orian, "Torrance, my boy, you will be all right. We will help you, and I assure you your mother and I are quite fine." This brought some comfort to the knight. Even though he wanted to free them, his thoughts turned to the dragons. They had to be freed first! Then another thought entered his mind: Plaitura. The imposter Morax had told him the people were safe because he, posing as Orian, and his mother were protecting the land. Now, he knew that was not the truth.

Plaitura was indeed in trouble. King Gavin awoke some three days ago to find his Kingdom shrouded in darkness and his people confused and frightened. The land was barren, with no vegetation, and the animals, too, were gone. Elders of Plaitura recalled when the King had been under the spell of Amiana and feared the worst. The King's knights stood ready for battle but did not know whom or what they were up against; nonetheless, they were prepared. King Gavin knew something was amiss when Torrance had failed to return from Scandos in a timely manner; he wondered where he was and if he was all right. He had promised his brother he would always take care of Torrance. He could not bear it if harm befell him. "How could I live with my decision to send him on a mission to help King Rufus and have something happen to him?" he spoke aloud. Chills ran through his body at the thoughts racing in his mind. "Please, Torrance, be safe and come home soon," the King said, his head in his hands. Sirs Michael, Anthony, and Kieran wondered what had become of their friend. They talked of better times when all was right with the land, almost as though they thought Torrance had succumbed to the forces that surrounded them. Sir Michael spoke up. "I am sure no harm has befallen our brother Knight, and we speak of him in the past." They all agreed that Torrance was not in harm's way. After all, he is an accomplished knight of Plaitura. King Gavin had a feeling that something was very, very wrong. Deep down, he knew the days of old were emerging once again. He felt a presence he had not felt in many years. The only word that came into his mind was Amiana. The King ordered his knights to be on guard for anything out of the ordinary. He still could not shake the feeling that harm had befallen Torrance. He had sent the young knight to his fate. He could not bear the thought of losing his beloved nephew. Tears started to stream down the King's face.

Morax began the battle, but the knight was unprepared. Torrance had been focusing on how to free his mother and Orian. He did not have time to defend himself, and again, he found himself on the ground dazed. As the Knight recovered from the blow Morax had hit him with, his mind became clearer. He now knew what to do. He had to free Armonious. She would restore balance just enough for Torrance to prepare for his counterattack.

Torrance knew now that the spells the imposter had taught him made the evil wizard stronger. "I must reverse them," he told himself. Everything became clearer to Torrance. He took the charm, placed it around his neck, and began to speak aloud. The Knight did not know where the words that were emerging from his lips were coming from. He charged forward with his sword drawn, chanting aloud. Morax's facial expression had changed. All of a sudden, he had a look of surprise and bewilderment. The knight held his sword high, charging toward the evil one. Fyndell jumped out in front of her master, and just as quickly as she came to his aide, she was on the ground, dazed from the blow. Morax stood fast, awaiting the blow he feared would be his demise. Torrance had devised this clever ruse, for his target was not the evil one who now stood in front of him. As Torrance held his sword high above his head, he turned to his left and struck the chains that held Armonious. His plan had worked. The mighty Armonious was free! As soon as she was freed, her color came back to her, and she soared high above the trees. Morax was mortified. "How could I have fallen for such an easy deception?" he asked aloud. "You," he said, pointing at Fyndell, who was still on the ground, dazed from the knight's blow. "You are useless," Morax screamed. "I am sorry, master," Fyndell said with her head bowed in shame. Then she looked up and replied defiantly, "You did not see that coming either."

Armonius roared with relief as she spread her wings after being bound for so long. She flew above the knight, and the most amazing sound emerged from her mighty jaw. It was a beautiful sound. Morax stood with his mouth slightly open from the expression on his evil face. You could tell he was not pleased. "How did you know which dragon to free first?" he asked the knight. Then, from out of the shadows, came a figure that gave the knight chills at the sight of her. It was Amiana. She had been watching from the shadows. She bowed her head as she came face-to-face with Morax and then asked, "Do you need my powers now, Master?" He replied, "I told you to stay out of sight until I summoned you." "I thought I could help after watching my sister being thrown to the ground." Morax looked angry as she spoke; clearly, they had a plan that now was not taking the course designed originally. Torrance felt a little sense of accomplishment watching the "mighty ones" in conflict with each other. That feeling was to be short-lived, for as he stood watching them, Amiana hit him with an unexpected blast that sent him almost over the edge of Zebulon. Torrance knew now he had to be prepared for anything and everything. "My boy, stand your ground. You can outsmart them," Orian's voice rang through the knight's mind. Then another voice came, "My son, I love you very much. We will help as much as we can." Torrance's mother was the voice in his head now, and he felt safe again.

Torrance watched as Armonius hovered above Zebulon. She looked very majestic with her wings spread, and now her color was back. The knight had never imagined he would be watching such a sight. As Torrance gazed at the dragon above him, he felt a glimmer of hope. That feeling was about to change drastically. He lost sight of the three evil powers he was facing for just a second. His mind was transfixed on how to free Orian and his mother. Amiana took advantage of the moment; she hit him with a jolt that knocked him to his knees. He was hurt but could not let Morax see his pain. He tried desperately to get to his feet. It was no use, he thought. I am done for. They will defeat me, he told himself. I will fail.

DAY
THIRTEEN

Torrance did not know what was happening to his beloved Plaitura. King Gavin and his fellow knights were facing evil also; Morax had sent others who were destroying the land. The people of Plaitura did not know what to do. They looked to their King for guidance; he brought everyone into the castle and armed them with swords and armor. He could only imagine where Torrance was. I am sorry, my brother. I have failed you, the King thought, for he knew if evil had plagued his castle, the surrounding lands would not be spared. His nephew must surely be dead by now. He had not heard any news of him since he had sent him to Scandos. King Gavin tried to shake the thought from his mind. He has a duty to his subjects to protect them. Armed with bows and swords, some of the King's knights lined the inner walls of the castle. They lie in wait for their enemy to approach. Sir Kieran, Sir Michael, and Sir Anthony stood fast in front of the other knights.

Although the people of Plaitura were facing what seemed to be their darkest moments, no one had been harmed. The evil presence just had them confined within the castle walls. King Gavin thought this was odd. "Why are they not attacking?" he asked aloud as if he was looking for someone to give him the answer he was seeking. His Knights were also baffled, but they still maintained their stance as defenders of Plaitura. Sir Kieran looked at his fellow knights. "What do we do now?" he asked. Sir Michael remained silent for a moment, then replied, "We do nothing until the King gives the command." Sir Anthony raised his sword and shouted, "Knights, stand ready. We fight on King Gavin's command!" They all raised their swords and cheered. They stood their ground waiting, but for what they did not know.

Elaina stood on her balcony, watching and wondering. She had bad feelings about the fate of her childhood companion, a companion whom she had grown to love, although she never let anyone know, including him, for she did not know how to tell him. She has loved him since they were children, and the older they grew, the more her love for him grew. They had shared almost their entire lives with each other. Now, she thought, "Should I have told him my true feelings?" A single tear fell from her eyes, thinking the worst. "I have to find him," she said aloud." "Find who?" one of the other chambermaids asked. She had just stepped into Elaina's room to ask her if she could stay with her, for she was afraid to be alone in her chambers. Her name is Isabelle; she and Elaina became friends. "No one," Elaina replied, "I was merely thinking aloud," Isabelle asked if she could stay in Elaina's chambers. "Of course, you may," Elaina said. "I would cherish the companionship," but in her mind, she really would have preferred to be alone. Elaina asked Isabelle if she would be all right for a moment while she went to the pantry to get something hot to drink. "It might calm us," she said as she exited her chambers. She did not intend to get them something to drink; in fact, Elaina only wanted to be alone with her thoughts. She went to Torrance's quarters instead and tried to focus her thoughts on the happier times when they were together, sharing their lives. In his quarters, she picked up a piece of his clothing and held it close to her heart. Does he know my true feelings, and are his the same? She wondered. Does he see us as just friends or more? She shook her head as if to disperse the thoughts forming in her mind. There are too many things to think of in this dark time. Why do I think of this now? she asked herself. The Kingdom was trapped by this presence, and the people did not know what to do! Elaina stood in the middle of the knight's quarters, feeling helpless. She walked onto the balcony, and by the looks of all the people, she could tell she was not alone.

A Sorceress standing on the castle wall watched the people of Plaitura and cast a spell. With her words came flashes of lightning and loud claps of thunder. The people drew back, ready to defend themselves, but none of the wizards or sorceresses advanced. The Kingdom was being held by fear and angst; no one was harmed. "Why do they not attack?" a man asked. Every time the evil group tried to pass the castle walls, they could not. It seemed as if there were invisible barriers that they could not penetrate.

Torrance regained his strength after Amiana's blow. He knew now he needed a different strategy if he were to succeed in freeing the dragons. In addition, the freedom of his mother and Orian weighed heavy on his mind. Armonious was circling the perimeter of Zebulon with soft sounds emanating from the dragon. He watched the dragon for a moment, and as he gazed at her, he felt a strange sensation. He felt revitalized. He rose to his feet, drew his sword, and advanced towards Morax. The evil wizard tried to stop the attack but could not. With a swipe of his blade, Torrance cut him. A small drop of blood oozed from the wound on the wizard's arm. Fyndell and Amiana shrieked in horror. They tried to defend their master but to no avail. "A lucky blow, young one," Morax taunted. Torrance's plan was not to kill the evil one but to distract him long enough to free another dragon. In reality, Torrance did not even know if a sword could defeat a wizard or if his demise would have to be by magic.

Orian communicated to Torrance, "You have to free the dragons. Time is short; forget about us." "I will free you all. That is my goal," Torrance answered. Morax, still seeping blood from his minor wound, started towards the knight with his staff. He held it in front of him, pointed it at the knight, and with a sweeping motion, the staff sent a bolt towards him. Oddly, the jolt had not touched Torrance. He felt sure this would be his demise as he awaited the blow. I am quite bewildered, he said to himself. How could a mage of his skill miss hitting me from such a close distance? "I am not wounded!" Torrance shouted. "You missed, old man!" Morax looked bewildered. How could he be unharmed? I was directly in front of him, and the jolt should have hit him. Then Fyndell and Amiana joined together and attacked the Knight using a combined spell, with no success. They were at a loss for words. "How can this be?" they shouted.

Torrance charged to his right, shouting the words of a spell the real Orian had taught him. Then, with a stroke of his blade, Ersella was free! Just as it was with Armonius, as soon as her bonds were broken and her color returned. She stretched her wings and took off for the sky. "Well done," Morax said, "You seem to have unseen forces protecting you." "I have no unseen forces, old man. You are just outmatched!" Torrance replied. Orian's voice pierced the Knight's thoughts, "Do not taunt him, my boy! He is stronger than you think!" Morax struck back hard, this time knocking the young knight right off the peak of the Mountain. As he was falling, he did not feel fear; he did not feel anything. Then, a strange feeling of calmness came over him. Was this how it felt to die? he wondered. Out of the corner of his eye, he saw something. It was Palmaro, only he was different. He was flying! He had wings. He positioned himself under Torrance and swooped him up back to the top of Zebulon. When they landed, Torrance patted his faithful horse and said, "I guess that is the reason I had a steady hand the day I won that contest. Thank you, boy, for being here," he stroked his head gently. Palmaro took off back to where they had made camp below the peak. I have seen strange things since meeting Orian, but I was not prepared for that, the knight said to himself. Morax and his evil daughters looked astonished as Palmaro flew away.

Morax decided to try to defeat the knight by hand-to-hand combat. He drew a sword and started towards Torrance. "You will not defeat me this way," Torrance said. "I am younger and quicker than you." With each cross of their swords, Lenore cringed. She closed her eyes, for she could not bear to watch as her son fought. Fearing the worst in her mind, she opened her eyes to see her son fighting skillfully. His hands were steady, strong, quicker, and more experienced than Morax. The knight had the upper hand now! The fight did not produce a favorable outcome, though. The two were at a standstill; neither one could defeat the other. Then, just as Morax was about to give up, Torrance sideswiped him, knocking the mage back just far enough to free Solarid. Just like the others, his color returned to normal, and he took to the sky. Torrance felt that with three of the dragons free, he might be able to complete his task successfully.

Torrance looked up for a moment, watching the dragons flying above, when he felt a sharp pain. Morax had taken advantage of the knight's distraction and sliced him across the upper arm. The old mage gloated, "So, I am old and slow? Your wound would prove otherwise." Though he was not mortally wounded, with only minimal blood loss, Torrance could not stop thinking about what could have happened. Now, more than ever, he had to focus. He could not let even the littlest thing distract him. Enraged, he turned to Morax and said, "I will show you just how old you are, mage." Torrance took his stance, and once again, their swords crossed. The air resounded with the scraping and clanging of metal. It was a sound that made Lenore quiver, but it excited the evil daughters. They fought blow for blow, with neither one coming any closer to ending the battle. Morax then summoned a spell. When Torrance heard the words, he knew how to protect himself against them. Fyndell decided to take matters into her own hands. She went after Lenore. The knight caught her advancing towards his mother, quickly shouted the spell to fend off Morax, and pushed him to the ground. He ran to intercept her. With his sword held high, he charged. He managed to get in front of her, and with a quick swipe of his blade, he cut her deeply across her abdomen. A loud scream emerged from her lips, and she fell to the ground, writhing in pain. Blood poured from her wound as she clutched her stomach, begging for help.

Morax's face turned ashen as he watched his daughter lying on the ground. Amiana shrieked in horror at the sight before her. Torrance stood fixed for a moment, watching as Fyndell lay on the ground. He quickly took advantage of the situation. While Morax and Amiana ran to the wounded Fyndell, he ran to free Hedradon and Myriel. The knight knew that freeing Nezaro would not be as easy; he was the strongest of the dragons, and his bonds were different than the others. Torrance smiled as he watched the dragons in flight. "So, you think the rest will be easy, do you?"

Morax asked with a cocky tone in his evil voice. "I am not through with you," he added. Torrance replied, "I seem to have the upper hand here," pointing to Fyndell lying on the ground bleeding. Amiana's facial expression turned from shock to a smirk. "She will not die from a mere blow of a sword, you foolish man," she said. "The amount of blood oozing from her body would prove otherwise," Torrance said. "Look again," Amiana said. He looked at the spot where the mortally wounded Fyndell lay, only to find she was no longer there. She was now standing beside Morax with not a scratch on her body. How can this be? What do I have to do to defeat them? Torrance asked himself. While the knight was deep in thought, the three attacked him. Now, it was Torrance on the ground in pain, waiting for the final blow. He could not move to defend himself. He just looked at the sky, watching the dragons flying.

Torrance heard the soft, sweet sound of Armonius and smiled at her. He then saw a single leaf floating downward from the trees, landing beside him. Torrance heard a familiar voice coming from the leaf and feared he was dying. He closed his eyes, and when he opened them, Elaina stood on the very spot where the leaf had landed. "Now I know I am dying," he whispered to himself. He felt a warm hand stroke his cheek. "You are not dying," Elaina reassured the knight. "How did you come to be here?" he asked. "I will explain all to you once you fulfill your quest," she replied, "but for now, all I ask of you is that you trust me." Torrance replied, "I trust you with all my heart and soul."

Orian sighed with relief when he saw Elaina standing beside the knight. "Now, all shall come together," Orian whispered to Lenore. She nodded her head and smiled in agreement. Elaina cast a spell of protection over Torrance until he regained his strength from the attack. It did not take him long to recover; he soon was standing at the side of his lifelong friend. He looked at her with awe and bewilderment. How did she come to be part of this? He asked himself. He thought back to their childhood. There had always been something special about

Elaina, but he did not know how special!

Torrance, fully recovered and joined by his childhood companion, now felt as though he could conquer the world! Elaina tried to distract the evil ones long enough to free Orian and Lenore. Torrance thanked Elaina for freeing his mother and Orian. This was one less thing he did not have to worry about, and he could focus on Nezaro and ending this battle.

Orian's voice rang out, "We will not be able to assist you, my boy. You have to finish this on your own." Torrance felt a knot in his stomach, "Am I strong enough?" he asked. "We will guide you as much as we can," his mother said, trying to ease her son's mind. Elaina grabbed hold of his hand, and the knot in his stomach eased. A peaceful and confident aura grew around him. He knew what he had to do now, though he did not know how he knew. It was all becoming very clear to the knight. He began having flashes in his mind of a similar battle. They were memories, not his own, but they were familiar to him somehow. Morax held his staff in front of him, and the more Torrance looked at it, the more things became clearer. He had seen it in the flashes he was having. The staff was made from the rib of the first and most powerful dragon of all, Noltac. This dragon possessed many powers. The first power was magic. Morax had slain Noltac for his powers, then took one of the dragon's ribs and infused his evil magic with the magic of Noltac. Without his staff, he could be defeated! Now, as the night gave way to a new day, Torrance felt the hope and confidence he needed!

DAY FOURTEEN

Torrance knew he held the key to separate the magic from the staff; the only problem he now faced was how to get it away from Morax. The key had been with him all along: the charm Orian had given him. Elaina looked at Torrance and nodded. She was ready. The knight smiled at her; he was ready to end this battle and return home to Plaitura. Torrance took a stance, drew his sword, raised it high above his head, and shouted, "Let us finish this, old man!" knowing his words would spark a rise out of Morax. The knight advanced towards the wizard as Elaina faked an attack on the evil daughters. Amiana and Fyndell looked surprised as Elaina came after them. "What does she think she can do to us?" Amiana asked her sister. "She cannot harm us," Fyndell answered. Elaina laughed at them. "So, you do not think I can harm you? Well, think again." Elaina shot a bolt of light out of her hand and clipped a tree branch. It fell in front of the sisters, and they watched as the branch landed at their feet. "That was just a warning," she boasted. "You are not untouchable." "I would not be so smug if I were you," Amiana said, readying herself to retaliate. Elaina turned quickly, held out her hand, and shouted, "I would not try it if I were you." The sisters looked at each other and decided not to attack Elaina. Instead, they turned their focus on the battle between Torrance and Morax. Torrance had to make his actions work to his benefit if he were to obtain the staff. He drew his sword, raised his shield, and charged towards the evil wizard. Morax was not prepared for this attack, and as the knight charged towards him, he had no time to defend himself. Torrance quickly knocked him off his feet onto the ground, and as he did this, the staff came loose from his hand. Fyndell tried to defend Morax but could not.

Everything was happening so fast that the evil ones did not know what to do. Torrance grabbed the staff and inserted the charm into it, just as the knight envisioned how it fit. Morax screamed a loud shrill as if he had been stabbed. "No!" he shrieked. "The staff is mine! You must not do that!" Torrance could feel the power surging through it. Rays of colors and light surrounded the knight. He knew his plan was working, and he could, at last, free Nezaro and finally go home. Drained both mentally and physically, Torrance wanted nothing more than to end this and return to Plaitura. The evil magic was still trying to control the staff, but the amulet prevented it from doing so. Suddenly, the staff let out a loud sound; it was the sound of a dragon's roar. It startled the knight, and he lost hold of the staff. It fell to the ground, and as it hit the ground, a shape began to form in front of the knight. It was the spirit of Noltac! Morax cringed in fear at the sight of him; he knew he was defeated. Torrance picked the staff up, pointed it at Nezaro, and broke the magical bindings that held him captive. Orian, Lenore, and Elaina cheered with joy and relief as Nezaro joined the other dragons. There was a moment when Nezaro and Noltac joined in flight before he joined the others. Noltac then disappeared into the clouds. The evil ones tried to escape off the Mountain while everyone was watching the dragons. Torrance stopped them with a powerful blast from the staff. He bound them with the magic of Noltac. He knew they were not stronger than him. It was a long, hard struggle for everyone, and now it was finally over! "My son, I am proud of you," Lenore said as she hugged her son. The other wizard and sorceress that held Plaitura at bay while the battle waged appeared on Zebulon and, like Morax and his daughters, were bound there. The magic of Noltac is so strong that it will hold them there indefinitely. Torrance now had possession of the staff, and it would not leave his sight.

Now, it was time to start the journey home. Torrance let out a sigh of relief and exhaustion. He was overjoyed as he watched the dragons flying above them as they made their way down the mountain to make their way home to Plaitura.

THE JOURNEY HOME

Now, at the bottom of the mountain, the four started out for home. Palmaro was ready to be mounted and whinnied as Torrance and Elaina climbed upon his back. Orian and Lenore mounted the other steed. The dragons, flying above them and keeping them in their sight, added a serene feeling to the weary knight. The land began to come back to life as they passed. The trees became green again, the flowers bloomed, and the animals and birds emerged as if to thank them as they rode by. "Now, my dear, how did you appear on the top of Zebulon?" Torrance asked Elaina. She smiled at the knight and said, "It was easy. I just thought of you, and there I was." She had a little smirk that was very vague on her face. Torrance said, "You are not telling me the whole truth, now are you." "My boy, I do not believe I have introduced you to my daughter," Orian said with a proud look. Torrance just laughed and said, "It does not surprise me. She has your eyes." Lenore just smiled. She knew everything would be as it should be, with Torrance next in line to be King and Elaina by his side as it always had been, and she could once again live in the land where she belonged and loved. It was a long trip back to Plaitura, but they did not stop much, only to water the horses and rest a bit. They could not wait to be home and restore the land to the days of old when all things were simple.

They were now passing Scandos. They stopped to make sure all was well with the people there. The fields were plentiful, the people were happy, and all was right. They dismounted the horses and led them to a stream so they could drink. King Rufus came to greet them. "I am happy to see you are all well," he said. "Stay and rest for a while; my cooks will prepare food for you." They accepted the invitation and stayed for a bit. They ate and drank and told the story of the conquest on the mountain. They were so anxious to return to Plaitura. They had not stopped for a long time, and the rest was refreshing. King Rufus looked up to the sky; seeing the dragons made him feel secure again. He knew now his people and land would be protected. His kingdom had not banished magic, and he knew all that was taking place. That is why Lenore had chosen to go there; she knew she did not have to hide her true self. Torrance and Orian knew it was time to make the last part of the journey home. They bid farewell to King Rufus and his people, mounted their horses, and followed the path to Plaitura.

When the people of Plaitura lost their protection, the people knew what was happening. They knew of the dragons and magic and knew their fate lay in the survival of the knight. The elders of Plaitura knew now that they could speak again of times unspoken of but not forgotten and started passing down stories of the dragons, wizards, and magic to the children. King Gavin also told the story of why magic was banished from their kingdom. Elaina and Torrance talked about their childhood, and she explained to him that she had no memory of who her Father was until the evil took hold of the kingdom. She told him she knew where she had to be and that it was by his side. He told her how happy he was that she appeared when she did. "I thought I would perish on the mountain and fail in my quest until I saw you by my side." Everyone was smiling and relieved when they saw the beautiful landscape and statues that led to Plaitura. The dragons, still flying high above them but not out of their sight, roared and swirled around each other playfully. The path they traveled came back to life as they flew past. Torrance admired the sight, and his heart filled with joy. Now, at their home, the people of the kingdom surrounded them; they were awestruck at the sight of the dragons! King Gavin came running to the knight's side. "I thought I had lost you, my boy," he said with tears streaming down his cheeks. He hugged him and then turned to Lenore and Orian. "Welcome home," he said with heartfelt sincerity. "There are not enough words to thank you for what you have done for all the people in all the lands! Then he turned to Elaina and said, "I always knew you were special, but I never thought you were the daughter of the greatest Wizard I have known." The knights surrounded Torrance. He was glad to see the faces of his friends. As he looked around, he spotted Sir Michael, Kieran, and Anthony. He grabbed them and held onto them, not wanting to let go. That night, King Gavin had a celebration prepared for the whole kingdom; Torrance told the story of how he defeated the evil Morax and his daughters. Orian regaled them with tales of the past.

Everyone had a story to tell while they ate and drank. Torrance took Elaina by the hand, walked her to his favorite spot, kissed her gently, and proclaimed his love for her. "You now and forever hold my heart," he said. She started to cry and replied, "You also now and forever hold my heart." They kissed deeply. They did not realize that they were in full view of all of Plaitura until they heard the cheers and applause of the people behind them. They returned to their place at the table, still holding each other's hands. Orian looked at Torrance and said, "There is one final task you must perform." He knew what he had to do. He held his staff high above his head, summoned the dragons, and commanded them to take their places. They did not hesitate. Each one of them came down lower and took their rightful places on the walls of the castle where they had been in the time of King Garrett and Queen Plaitura. Nezaro took the highest pillar, Armonious took the center of the garden, Myreil took the right front side of the outer wall, Hedradon took the left side, and on the back pillars proudly sat Ersella on the right side, and Solarid on the left. "Now all is as it should be," Orian proclaimed. "The dragons are yours now. They will protect you and obey you." The kingdom of Plaitura was restored, and the people would be as they once were: content. The dragons took their rightful place as The Protectors of the Knight.

THE END

www.ingramcontent.com/pod-product-compliance
Lightning Source LLC
Chambersburg PA
CBHW061138200626
46817CB00016B/1966